Good Morning, River!

By Lisa Westberg Peters
Illustrated by Deborah Kogan Ray

Arcade Publishing · New York

LITTLE, BROWN AND COMPANY

"Good morning!"

Katherine heard the old man's voice boom out across the broad river valley. A softer voice called back, "Good morning . . . good morning. . . ."

The old man was Carl. He was Katherine's friend. He always told Katherine that the softer voice was the river talking back to him.

"That's silly," Katherine would say. "The river can't talk." Then she would shout in a squeaky voice, "Good morning!" No voice ever called back.

"See?" Katherine would say. "The river doesn't talk to me."

"Maybe someday it will," he'd say.

After breakfast, Katherine ran to Carl's house. It was time to check the river's ice. They climbed down the bluff and saw thick slabs of ice curled over the shore as if they had frozen in the middle of a wave. Carl walked out and bounced a few times.

Then Katherine stepped out. Crunch, one foot. Crunch, the other foot.

They crouched down and brushed away the white snow. Dark ice, full of ripples, bubbles, and cracks, lay beneath.

"How can you tell it's safe to walk on?" Katherine asked.

The ice rumbled gently. "The river tells me," Carl said with a wink. Katherine listened again, but she heard nothing.

The winter passed. The river was swollen with snow melt and rain. Floodwater rose to the limbs of the trees, and everywhere was the sweet smell of rotting leaves.

Carl marked Katherine's height on his wooden cane and said, "You're a half inch taller, Miss Katherine. That's big enough for a jungle ride."

They climbed into the red canoe. Carl pretended he was dizzy with jungle fever, and Katherine pretended she was sweaty in the steamy rain.

"Watch out for alligators and snakes," she warned. He paddled around them.

Katherine listened for jungle sounds and heard a soft chuckle. "It's a monkey!" she cried. But when she looked for it, all she saw was the river rushing past their canoe.

Spring turned to summer, and the floodwater drew back. The river sparkled in hot white sunlight, and shimmery heat rose from the sand.

One afternoon, Katherine lost her first tooth. Carl reached into his pocket and gave her two nickels—a shiny one as old as she, and a smooth one as old as he.

"Been saving these for you," he said. "You're growing up. In fact, I'll bet you can swim all the way to the dock this year."

"I don't want to," she said. "I might bump into a turtle."

"I used to swim underwater with my eyes wide open," Carl said. "Never bumped into a thing."

Katherine decided to try. She held her breath, opened her eyes, and stared into the watery darkness. "Hello!" she shouted, but the word bubbled up to the surface and popped.

After her swim, she sat on the beach with Carl and sang her favorite songs. The river answered with its own music—a steady slap . . . slap . . . slap of the evening ripples. Carl didn't sing. He was asleep.

In the fall, a steady wind began to blow across the river. It whipped the waves into gray peaks and tossed their foamy caps into the air.

One morning, Katherine didn't hear Carl's booming voice, just the dry scratch of branches against the glass. She left her breakfast and ran through the woods to his house.

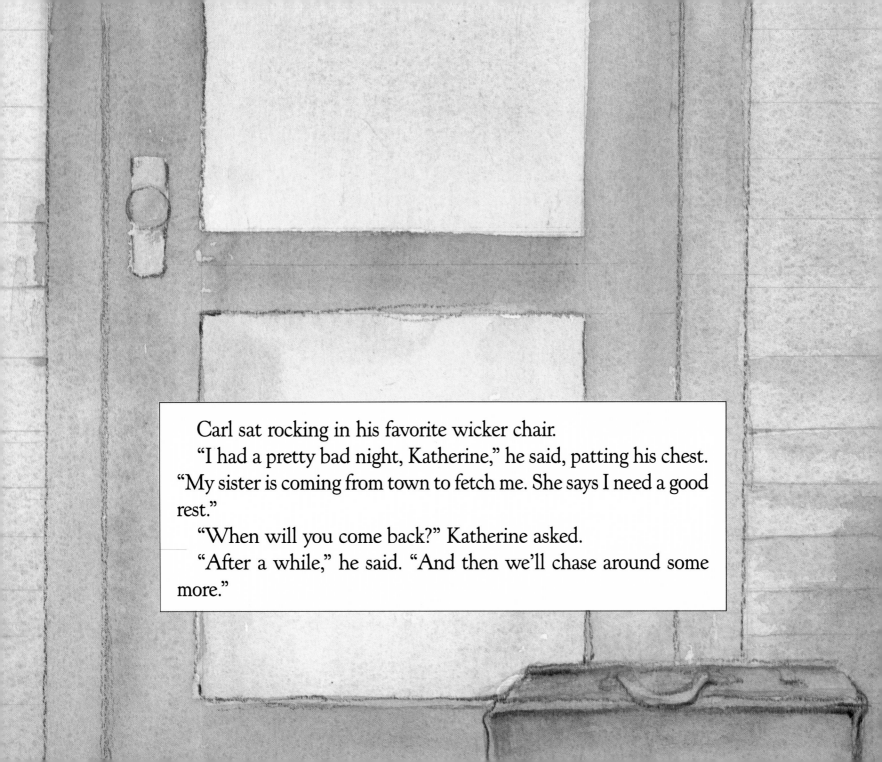

Carl sat rocking in his favorite wicker chair.

"I had a pretty bad night, Katherine," he said, patting his chest. "My sister is coming from town to fetch me. She says I need a good rest."

"When will you come back?" Katherine asked.

"After a while," he said. "And then we'll chase around some more."

Katherine stayed until Carl's sister came. The car disappeared in the dust of the gravel road.

All that fall, the cold drizzle chilled the chickadees into silence. The river was silent, too.

It froze over one day with a thin skin of ice. No ripples, no bubbles, no cracks. That was the day Carl came home.

Katherine saw the smoke from his chimney and raced to see him. There he was, rocking in his wicker chair, but something was different. His booming voice was gone. "I don't think I can say good morning to the river today," he whispered.

Katherine hesitated. "Maybe I can," she said.

She turned to face the broad valley, stood tall, and held her hands around her mouth. As loudly as she could, Katherine yelled, "Good morning!"

And she heard the river answer. A softer voice called back, "Good morning . . . good morning. . . ."

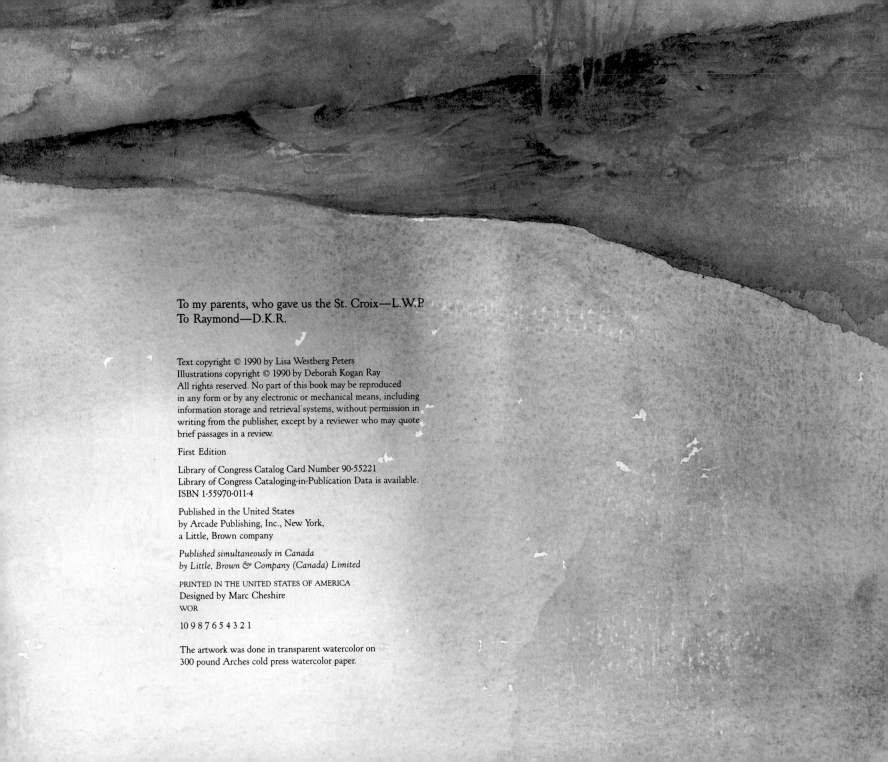

Text copyright © 1990 by Lisa Westberg Peters
Illustrations copyright © 1990 by Deborah Kogan Ray

First Edition

Library of Congress Catalog Card Number 90-55221
Library of Congress Cataloging-in-Publication Data is available.
ISBN 1-55970-011-4

Published in the United States
by Arcade Publishing, Inc., New York,
a Little, Brown company

*Published simultaneously in Canada
by Little, Brown & Company (Canada) Limited*

PRINTED IN THE UNITED STATES OF AMERICA
Designed by Marc Cheshire
WOR

10 9 8 7 6 5 4 3 2 1

The artwork was done in transparent watercolor on
300 pound Arches cold press watercolor paper.